D0518249

Dedicated to:

Carlos and Loretta Spaht

KING OF THE MOUNTAIN

© copyright 1998 by ARO Publishing.
All rights reserved, including the right of reproduction in whole or
in part in any form. Designed and produced by ARO Publishing.
Printed in the U.S.A. P.O. Box 193 Provo, Utah 84603

ISBN 0-89868-356-4–Library Bound
ISBN 0-89868-411-0–Soft Bound
ISBN 0-89868-357-2–Trade

A PREDICTABLE WORD BOOK

KING OF THE MOUNTAIN

Story by Janie Spaht Gill, Ph.D.
Illustrations by Bob Reese

 ARO PUBLISHING

Once there was a lion who was very, very proud. He stood on the mountain top and roared out very loud,

4

"My roar is fierce, my claws are grand. I am the king of all the land."

A voice answered back, "My roar is fierce, my claws are grand. I am king of all the land."

The lion was surprised that there was another as great as he, so he growled as loudly as could be, "Listen to my roar – R-r-r-o-a-r-r. You cannot out do that!"

But the voice answered back equally as loud, "Listen to my roar – R-r-r-o-a-r-r. You cannot out do that!"

The lion became angry and growled, "Who are you to challenge me?"

But the voice answered back, "Who are you to challenge me?"

11

The lion called out, "I'll meet you in the valley. There we will decide who is the greatest."

The voice answered back, "I'll meet you in the valley. There we will decide who is the greatest."

And so, the lion pranced down to the valley.

In the valley there was a beautiful stream.

The lion looked in the water and saw a lion looking back at him.

The lion roared his mighty roar and showed his great claws. The lion in the water roared his mighty roar and showed his great claws.

"Very well," said the lion. "Your roar is fierce, your claws are grand. The two of us shall rule the land."

Now when the lion stands on top of the mountain and roars his terrible roar, he waits for the voice of another who answers just like before.

For the lion has found that no matter how great he thinks himself to be, somewhere there's another lion that's just as great as he.